Who Gets the Sun Out of Bed?

Who Gets the Sun Out of Bed?

WRITTEN BY

Nancy White Carlstrom

ILLUSTRATED BY

David McPhail

Little, Brown and Company

Boston   Toronto   London

For two boys and a bunny named Midnight
— N. W. C.

For Maria, who made me do it
— D. M.

Text copyright © 1992 by Nancy White Carlstrom
Illustrations copyright © 1992 by David McPhail

First Edition

Library of Congress Cataloging-in-Publication Data

Carlstrom, Nancy White.
    Who gets the sun out of bed? / written by Nancy White Carlstrom ;
illustrated by David McPhail. — 1st ed.
        p.   cm.
    Summary: Although the lazy sun is reluctant to rise, one by one
the members of a cozy household get up.
    ISBN 0-316-12862-7 (lib. bdg.)
    [1. Sun — Fiction.   2. Morning — Fiction.]   I. McPhail, David M.,
ill.   II. Title.
PZ7.C21684Who   1992
[E] — dc20   91-32313

10 9 8 7 6 5 4 3 2 1

NIL

Published simultaneously in Canada
by Little, Brown & Company (Canada) Limited

Printed in Italy

IN THE COLD, DARK WINTER,
who gets the sun out of bed?

Not the spruce tree,
sighing softly in the starlight.

Not the stars,
winking gently over the house.

Not the house,
snoring peacefully under the blanket
of new snow.

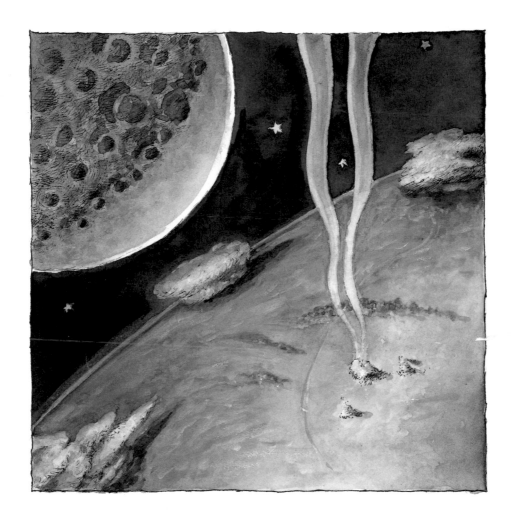

Not the snow,
shining silvery beneath the lingering moon.

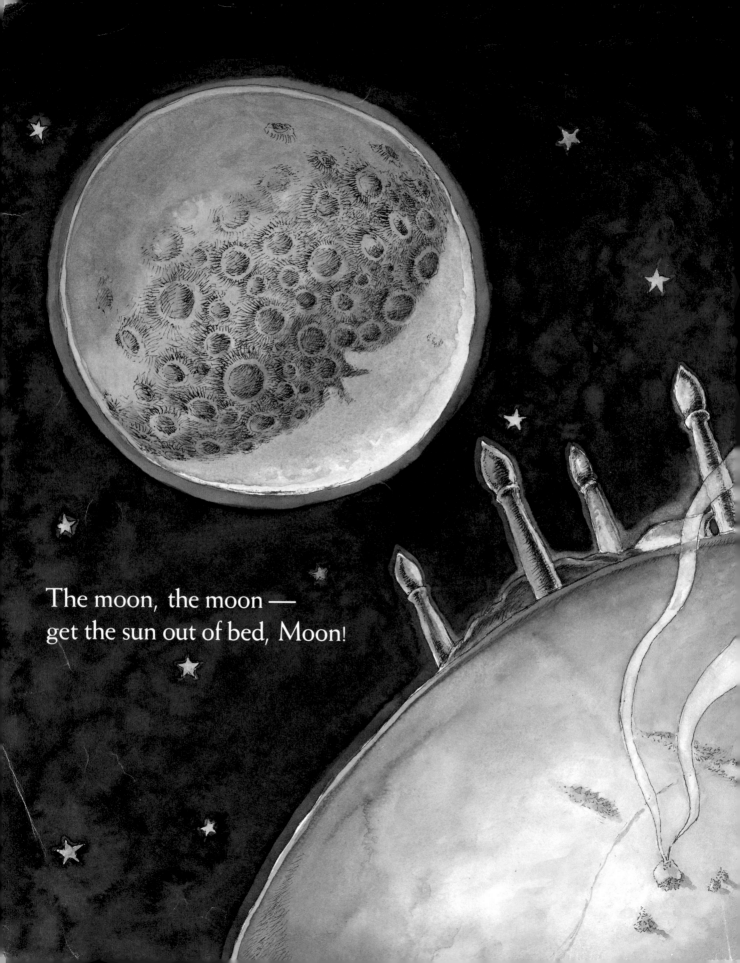

The moon, the moon —
get the sun out of bed, Moon!

IN THE COLD, DARK WINTER,
who gets the sun out of bed?

Not the fire,
glowing red in the stove.

Not the stove,
staying hot under the kettle.

Not the kettle,
whispering near the bed of a bunny
named Midnight.

The bunny, the bunny —
get the sun out of bed, Midnight!

IN THE COLD, DARK WINTER,
who gets the sun out of bed?

Not the wind,
knocking boldly at the door.

Not the door,
 keeping out the waking wolves.

Not the wolves,
howling a long way off from the little
boy's room.

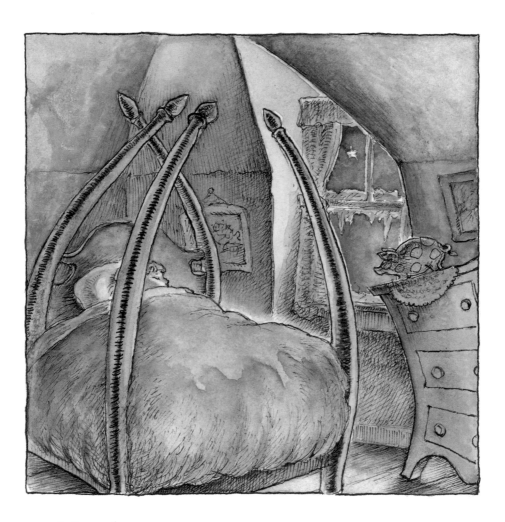

Not the room,
wrapping its arms around the little boy
named Nicholas.

The boy, the boy —
get the sun out of bed, Nicholas!

IN THE COLD, DARK WINTER,
who gets the sun out of bed?

The moon nudges the bunny
named Midnight.

The bunny hops into the room
of the little boy named Nicholas.

She jumps up onto his bed
and kisses him on the nose.

Nicholas stretches and yawns.
He hugs the bunny
and carries her out of his room.

Together they stand at the window.
The bunny perks up her ears and wiggles her nose.

The moon waits patiently at the crest of the hill.

Then Nicholas shouts,
"Good morning, Sun!
Get out of bed!"

The sun opens one eye,
raises its head, and says,

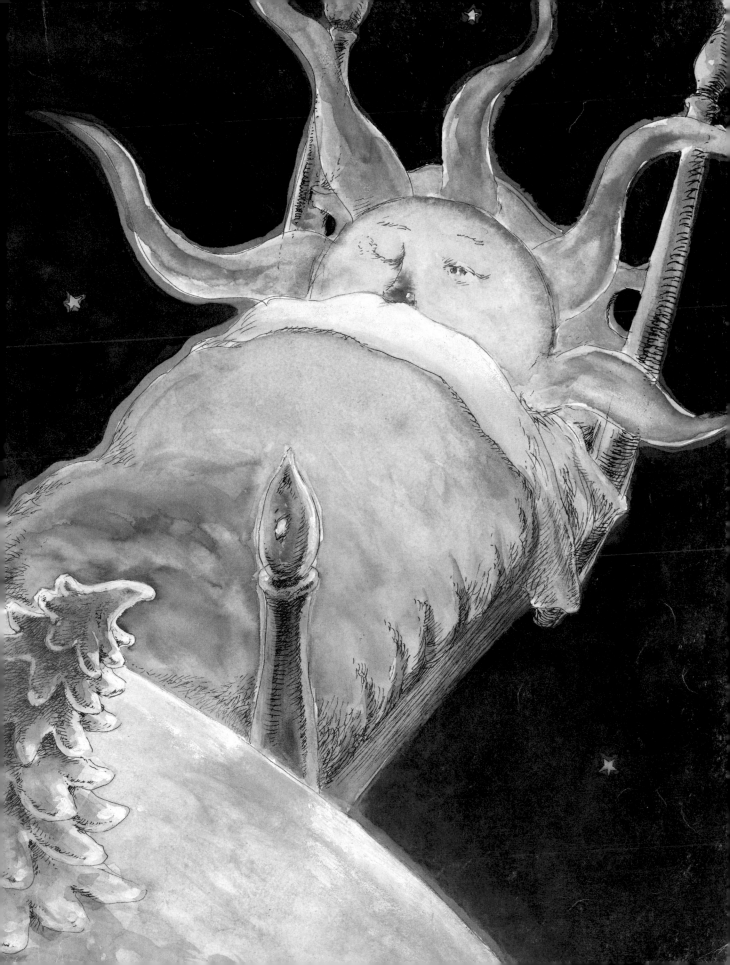

"Good morning, Moon!
Good morning, Nicholas!
Good morning, Midnight!"